This book belongs to

....

Walt Disney's

The Jungle Book

Storybook Favourites

Reader's Digest Young Families

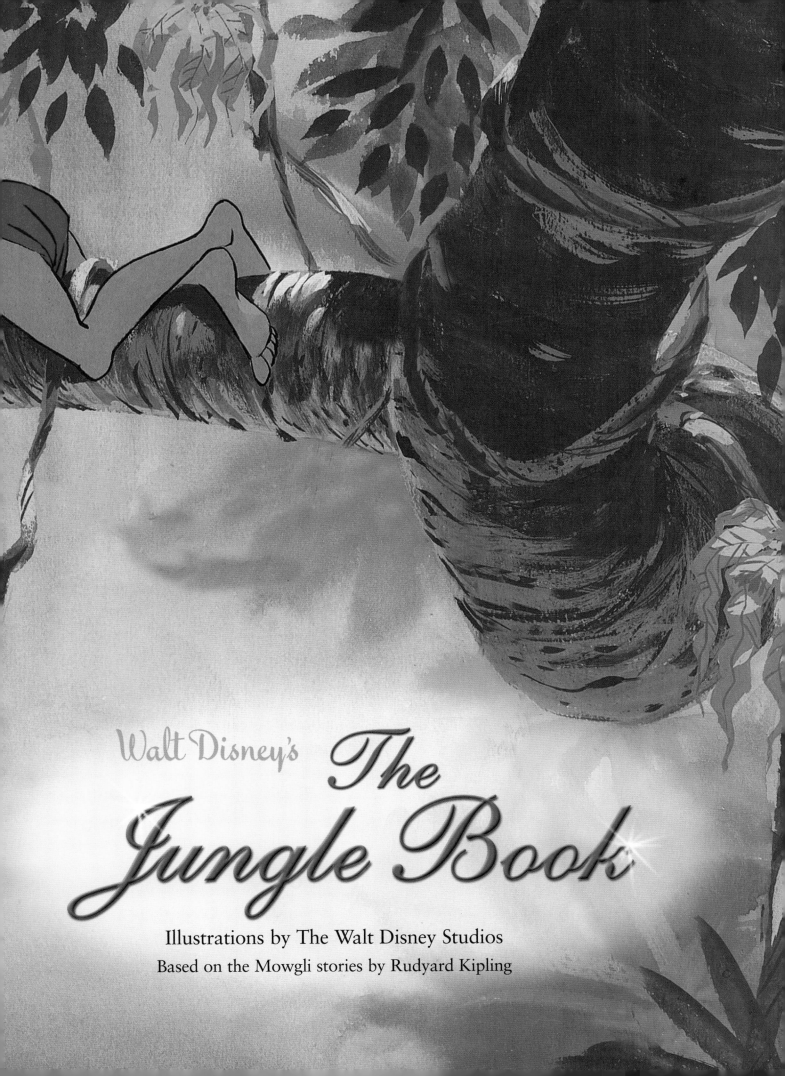

Walt Disney's *The Jungle Book*

Illustrations by The Walt Disney Studios

Based on the Mowgli stories by Rudyard Kipling

$\mathcal{M}$any strange legends are told of the jungles of far-off India. They speak of Bagheera, the black panther, and of Baloo the bear. They tell of Kaa, the sly python, and of the Lord of the Jungle, the great tiger, Shere Khan. But of all the legends, none is so strange as the story of a small boy named Mowgli.

The story began when a child, left all alone in the jungle, was found by Bagheera the panther. He could not give the small, helpless 'Man-cub' care and nourishment, so Bagheera took him to the den of a wolf family with young cubs of their own.

That is how it happened that Mowgli, as the Man-cub came to be called, was raised among the wolves. All the jungle folk were his friends.

Bagheera took Mowgli on long walks and taught him jungle lore.

Baloo, the bumbling bear, played games with Mowgli and taught him to live a life of ease. There were coconuts to crack, bananas to peel, and sweet and juicy pawpaws to pick from the jungle trees.

Hathi, the proud old leader of the elephant herd, tried to train young Mowgli to march along in military style as he led his troop trumpeting down the jungle trails.

Sly old Kaa the python would have loved to squeeze Mowgli tight in his coils. Mowgli's friends warned him against Kaa.

It was Shere Khan the tiger who was the real danger to Mowgli. That was because Shere Khan, like all tigers, had a hatred of man.

Ten times the season of rains had come to the jungle while Mowgli made his home with the wolf family. Then Shere Khan returned to the wolves' hunting grounds.

The wolf pack met at Council Rock when next the moon was full.

'As you know,' said Akela, the leader of the pack, 'Shere Khan the tiger has returned. If he learns that our pack is looking after a Man-cub, danger will be doubled for all our families. Are we agreed that the Man-cub must go?'

Out of the shadows stepped Bagheera the panther. 'I brought the Man-cub to the pack,' he said. 'It is my duty to see him safely out of the jungle. I know a Man-village not far away where he will be well-cared for.'

So it was arranged, and when the greenish light of the jungle morning slipped through the leaves, Bagheera and Mowgli set out.

All day they walked, and when night fell they slept on a high branch of a giant banyan tree. All this seemed like an adventure to Mowgli. But when he learned that he was to leave the jungle, he was horrified.

'No!' cried Mowgli. 'The jungle is my home.
I can take care of myself. I will stay!'
He slipped down a length of trailing vine and
ran away.

For a while Mowgli marched with Hathi and the elephants. But he soon tired of that.

Then he found Baloo bathing in a jungle pool. Mowgli joined him for a dip.

Suddenly down swooped the monkey folk. They had snatched Mowgli from the pool before Baloo knew what was happening.

They tossed him through the air from hand to hand, and swung him away through the trees.

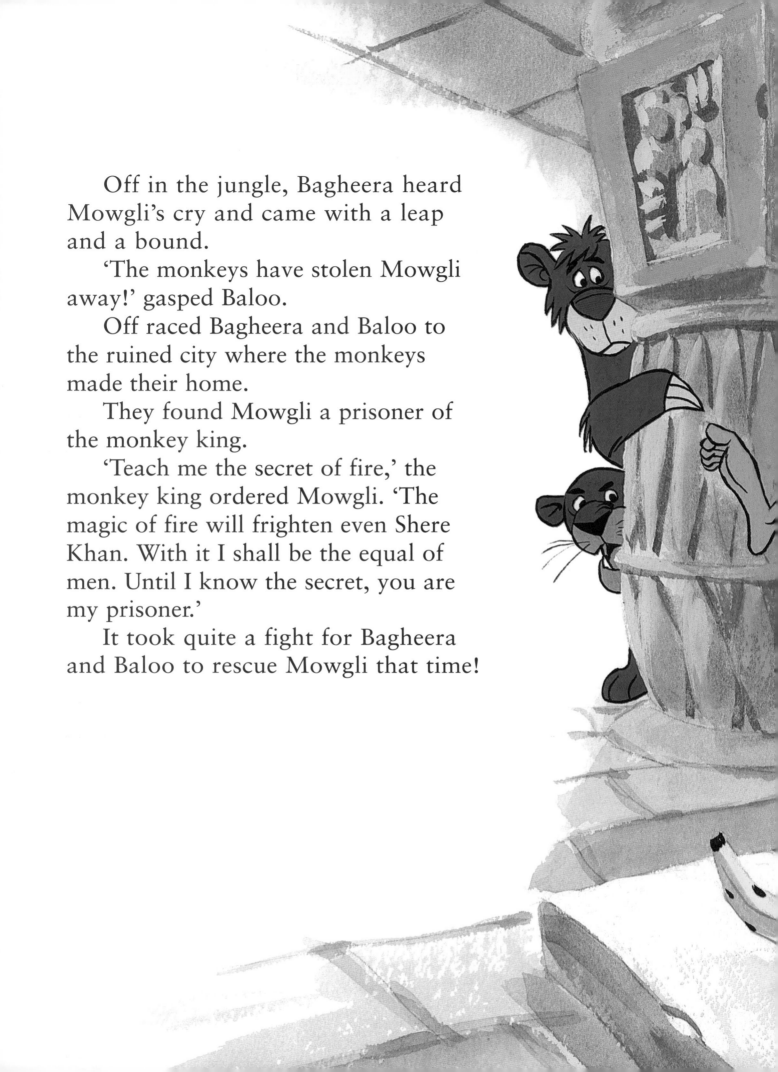

Off in the jungle, Bagheera heard Mowgli's cry and came with a leap and a bound.

'The monkeys have stolen Mowgli away!' gasped Baloo.

Off raced Bagheera and Baloo to the ruined city where the monkeys made their home.

They found Mowgli a prisoner of the monkey king.

'Teach me the secret of fire,' the monkey king ordered Mowgli. 'The magic of fire will frighten even Shere Khan. With it I shall be the equal of men. Until I know the secret, you are my prisoner.'

It took quite a fight for Bagheera and Baloo to rescue Mowgli that time!

'Now you see,' they told him, 'why you must go to the Man-village to be safe.'

But alas, that foolish boy would not understand. He kicked up his heels and ran away again.

This time his wanderings led him to where Shere Khan lay waiting in the high grass, smiling a hungry smile.

When Mowgli caught sight of the tiger, Shere Khan asked, 'Well, Man-cub, aren't you going to run?'

But Mowgli did not know that he should be afraid. 'Why should I run?' he asked, staring Shere Khan in the eye as the tiger gathered himself ready to spring. 'I'm not afraid of you.'

'That foolish boy!' growled Bagheera, who had crept close just in time to hear Mowgli.

Both Bagheera and Baloo flung themselves upon Shere Khan, to save Mowgli once more.

They were brave and strong, but the tiger was mighty of tooth and claw.

There was a flash of lightning, and a dead tree nearby caught fire. Mowgli snatched a burning branch and waved it in Shere Khan's face. The tiger, terrified, ran away. Mowgli was very pleased with himself as he strutted between the two weary warriors, Bagheera and Baloo.

Suddenly Mowgli stopped. From ahead came a sound that was strange to him. He peeked through the brush. It was the song of a village girl who had come to fill her water jar.

As he listened to the soft notes of her song, Mowgli felt strange inside. He felt that he must follow her. Mowgli crept up the path to the village, enthralled by the girl and her song.

Baloo and Bagheera watched the two figures as long as they could be seen. When Mowgli vanished inside the village gate, Bagheera sighed a deep sigh.

'It is just as it should be, Baloo,' he said. 'Our Mowgli is safe in the Man-village at last. He has found his true home.'

Walt Disney's The Jungle Book is a *Disney Storybook Favourites* book

Walt Disney's The Jungle Book, copyright © 1967, 2005 Disney Enterprises, Inc.
Illustrations by The Walt Disney Studios.
Based on the Mowgli stories in *The Jungle Book* and *The Second Jungle Book* by Rudyard Kipling.

This edition was adapted and published in 2009 by
The Reader's Digest Association Limited
11 Westferry Circus, Canary Wharf, London E14 4HE

Editor: Rachel Warren Chadd
Designer: Louise Turpin
Design consultant: Simon Webb

® Reader's Digest, the Pegasus logo and Reader's Digest Young Families
are registered trademarks of
The Reader's Digest Association, Inc.

We are committed both to the quality of our products
and the service we provide to our customers.
We value your comments, so please do contact us on
08705 113366 or via our website at
www.readersdigest.co.uk
If you have any comments or suggestions
about the content of our books, email us at
gbeditorial@readersdigest.co.uk

Printed in China

A Disney Enterprises/Reader's Digest Young Families Book

ISBN 978 0 276 44466 1
Book code 641-025 UP0000-1
Oracle code 504400016H.00.24